BAD LUCK SKATE

HARDY BOYS

→Clue Book←

#14

BAD LUCK SKATE

BY FRANKLIN W. DIXON ⇄ ILLUSTRATED BY SANTY GUTIÉRREZ

ALADDIN

NEW YORK   LONDON   TORONTO   SYDNEY   NEW DELHI

ALADDIN

An imprint of Simon & Schuster Children's Publishing Division
1230 Avenue of the Americas, New York, NY 10020
First Aladdin hardcover edition August 2021
Text copyright © 2021 by Simon & Schuster, Inc.
Illustrations copyright © 2021 by Santy Gutiérrez
Also available in an Aladdin paperback edition.

For information about special discounts for bulk purchases, please contact
Simon & Schuster Special Sales at 1-866-506-1949 or business@simonandschuster.com.
The Simon & Schuster Speakers Bureau can bring authors to your live event.
For more information or to book an event contact the Simon & Schuster Speakers Bureau
at 1-866-248-3049 or visit our website at www.simonspeakers.com.
Series designed by Karina Granda
Jacket designed by Tiara Iandiorio
The illustrations for this book were rendered digitally.
The text of this book was set in Adobe Garamond Pro.
Manufactured in the United States of America 0721 FFG
2 4 6 8 10 9 7 5 3 1
Library of Congress Cataloging-in-Publication Data
Names: Dixon, Franklin W., author. | Gutiérrez, Santy, 1971- illustrator. |
Title: The bad luck skate / Franklin W. Dixon ; illustrated by Santy Gutiérrez. |
Description: First Aladdin hardcover edition. | New York : Aladdin, [2021] | Series: Hardy Boys
clue book ; 14 | Audience: Ages 6 to 9. | Summary: Bayport Elementary's detective brothers Frank
and Joe Hardy are on the case when someone sabotages the hockey team's lucky charm right
before the championship game.
Identifiers: LCCN 2020029211 (print) | LCCN 2020029212 (ebook) |
ISBN 9781534460218 (pbk) | ISBN 9781534460225 (hc) | ISBN 9781534460232 (ebook)
Subjects: CYAC: Luck—Fiction. | Hockey—Fiction. | Brothers—Fiction. |
Mystery and detective stories.
Classification: LCC PZ7.D644 Bad 2021 (print) | LCC PZ7.D644 (ebook) | DDC [Fic]—dc23
LC record available at https://lccn.loc.gov/2020029211

CONTENTS

THE COOLEST SPORT IN THE WORLD

"Hey, Frank," Pete Peterson called, slinging his hockey bag over his shoulder. "Here to watch the big game?"

Nine-year-old Frank Hardy gave his friend a fist bump. "I wouldn't miss it for the world," he said.

"I thought you said Pete was as big as a giant," blurted Frank's eight-year-old brother, Joe. He had tagged along to watch Pete's team, the Bayport Checkers, play in the division hockey championship against the Southport Snipers. Frank and Joe didn't play hockey, but they both loved supporting their friends.

"I didn't say Pete was 'as big as a giant,'" Frank replied. "I said he *played* like one."

The beginning of the Checkers' season had been rough. They'd lost five of their first six games. The players hadn't been passing to one another. They couldn't score goals. No one was having fun. That had all changed in October, when Pete moved to town. With his stellar play and leadership, the team had managed to turn their season around by winning thirteen of their last fifteen.

Not only was Pete a whiz on the ice, but he was the kind of kid everyone liked. He and Frank had become friends at school. Over the past few months, Frank had been to most of Pete's games, and he was looking forward to watching his friend win a championship.

"Pete's not just the team captain," Frank told his brother. "He's the best player in the league."

"Shucks, Frank," Pete said. "I'm only as good as the team around me."

Frank and Joe knew a lot about being a good team. Working together, a good team could accomplish anything they put their minds to. And what the brothers put their minds to best was solving mysteries.

The boys' dad, Fenton Hardy, ran his own detective agency in Bayport. Frank and Joe liked to think they were carrying on the family business, solving mysteries of their own. They wrote down everything about their cases, including suspects and clues, in their clue book. The brothers carried it everywhere they went. You never knew when a mystery might pop up.

"Out of the way, goon," a girl called from behind the boys. The girl was Joe's age. She had white skates slung over her shoulder, her hair done up in a ponytail, and she was dragging a small suitcase.

Pete rolled his eyes. "My sister, Pam," he told the boys. "She has a figure-skating competition on the other rink."

"Hi, Pam," called Joe. "I didn't know you skated."

"The whole family does," Pam responded. "Not that anyone ever watches my skating competitions.

They're too busy watching Pete sniff his skates before every hockey game."

"I do not *sniff my skates*," Pete protested.

"That's a good thing," Joe said, waving a hand in front of his nose. "The smell is bad enough with the skates still in your bag."

"You might not be all about the stink," Pam argued, "but you're still weird before you play."

Pete gave his sister a hard look. "I have a game-day routine. It helps get me focused and ready to play."

"Exactly," Frank agreed. "All the best athletes have one. Following a steady game-day routine programs your body to perform when you need it to. That way, you can focus on the important thing— getting a win."

"You can call it a routine," Pam said. "I call it superstition. Every little thing needs to be *exactly* the same or he has a hissy fit and makes a big deal about how they won't win."

"Not every little thing." Pete frowned. "There are just a few steps I take that help me play better. The way I tape my stick, for instance. If I use black tape, it hides the puck, making it harder for the goalie to see. And I leave the top hole on my skates unlaced to help me get lower when I skate."

"That all sounds practical," Frank said.

"He left out the part about sniffing the stinky skate," Pam said, smiling a devilish grin.

Pete looked away. "There is one superstition," he confessed. "But it doesn't involve smelling anything."

Everyone stared at Pete, waiting for him to

continue. It was obvious he was a little embarrassed. "We always touch our lucky skate before taking the ice. It started as a way to bring the team together. The one time we didn't do it, we lost 4–0."

"Eww," Joe said, waving his hand in front of his nose again. "Touch a smelly skate or lose the game? That's a tough choice."

Pete shrugged. "I'll do anything to help us win."

They were about to head into the rink when a deep voice interjected, "I hope that includes cleaning up after yourself, young man."

The kids all turned in the direction of the speaker, a large man dressed in faded blue overalls, who was wagging a finger in Pete's direction.

"Hey, Wally," Pete said, waving at the rink's maintenance man.

"There's a lot going on in there today," Wally continued. "I'll have enough to do without you boys making any more messes."

"We'll be good," Pete promised.

"Morning, Wally." Pam waved.

Wally waved back. "Big competition for you

today, little lady. Win this, and you could get a spot at nationals. I'm sure there's going to be a big crowd."

Pam frowned. "The division hockey championship is today. That's where the crowds will be."

"Plenty of folks know how amazing you figure skaters are," Wally reassured her. "I bet your parents can't wait to watch."

"They've got to stop by Gram's house today," Pam grumbled. "They're gonna try to make it back, but who knows."

"I know I'll be there," Wally responded.

"I'd like to watch you skate too," added Joe. "Frank will definitely come with me. Just let us know when you go on."

"Thanks, guys," Pam said. "I'll find out what time my competition starts, but I'm sure it will overlap with Pete's game. Everyone will be over there. That's what always happens."

"We'll make it," Joe promised, but Pam was already walking away.

Chapter 2.

THE GOON SQUAD

While Frank went with Pete to drop his hockey equipment in the locker room, Joe wandered toward the café. He figured there might be some tasty treats there. Even if there weren't any snacks, he had time to kill. Maybe he'd run into someone else he knew from school.

The café was set up between the rinks. Two big windows on each side let spectators look onto the ice. There were small tables along one wall near the windows, but they were all empty. Joe headed past the seating area to the main counter at the front.

As it turned out, there weren't many snack options to choose from. Joe was busy looking them over when someone crashed into him from behind.

"So sorry for bumping you," said a flustered boy a little bigger than Joe. He was stumbling, overloaded with hockey equipment, including a large set of goalie pads. The boy fidgeted from foot to foot and, upon close inspection, appeared to be sweating. All in all, he seemed kind of out of control.

"No damage done," Joe said, waving off the apology. He smiled reassuringly.

The boy stared at Joe for an uncomfortable minute before adjusting his glasses and asking, "Hey, you're Frank's brother, aren't you?"

"That's me. Joe Hardy, at your service."

"Nice to meet you. I'm Freddy," the boy said, dropping his gear and offering his hand.

Yep, definitely sweaty, Joe thought as he shook Freddy's hand. *He must be nervous.* Joe was good at picking up on those little details. It was a necessary skill for any detective.

But *why* was Freddy so nervous and sweaty?

"Is everything okay?" Joe asked.

Freddy shuffled his feet and glanced around. "Our number one goalie is home with the flu. Coach just told me I'm in net for the championship. 'Mercer,' he said, 'you've got the start for the Checkers today.' But I'm not ready to start. Not a game this big."

"Didn't you say your name was Freddy?" Joe asked. He really was good at picking up on little details.

"Yeah. My first name's Freddy. Coach calls me Mercer because our other goalie's name is also Freddy. It got confusing there for a while."

"I can imagine." Joe laughed. It was getting confusing now, too.

"Do you play?" Freddy asked, gesturing to the hockey bag he'd dropped on the floor.

"Nah," Joe admitted. "I'm more of a baseball guy. I'm here with Frank to watch the game."

"If there even *is* a game," Freddy grumbled. "I'm not sure I can do this."

The poor goalie thumped down at one of the café tables. Freddy really looked miserable. Joe thought back to his last baseball game. He'd been at bat in the final inning. They were down by one. A hit could help the team win, but an out would lose the whole thing.

Was that the same pressure that Freddy was under now? Maybe Joe could help.

Joe didn't know much about hockey. He figured it basically came down to putting the puck in the net. This made the goalie a pretty important part of the team. And Joe did know something about that. Not only was he an important part of his baseball team, but he was also half of the Hardy brothers detective team. Frank was great at helping build Joe's confidence. And that was what Freddy needed. Confidence.

"This is what you practice for," Joe said. "I'm sure you'll be great. After all, the coach is confident enough to put you in net, right?"

"It's not like he has any other options," Freddy replied.

"Hockey is a team game. You're not out there on your own. Your team will be there for you."

"Winning is about who scores more goals," Freddy said. "What if I let one in?"

"With a five hole as big as yours, you'll let in way more than one," taunted a voice from behind Joe.

Unfortunately, Joe knew that voice, so he wasn't surprised when he and Freddy turned to find Bayport Elementary's biggest bully, fourth-grader Adam Ackerman. Joe felt his heart drop. Of course Adam would show his face just when Freddy was close to cheering up.

"Can't wait to watch my boys put pucks past you, Mercer," Adam jeered. "How many did they score on you last game? Six?"

Freddy gritted his teeth. "Actually, I wasn't in net for that game."

Adam let out a big laugh. "Yeah. If you had been, the loss would have been much worse."

Joe saw Freddy starting to wilt under Adam's taunts.

If there was one thing Joe couldn't stand, it was a bully. "Why don't you just leave him alone? At least he's play-ing in the game. That's more than you can say."

Freddy chuckled, while Adam glowered but said nothing.

"You think you know everything, don't you?" he finally grumbled.

"I know you weren't good enough to make the Checkers," Freddy said. "Or the Snipers." It seemed like he was feeling more confident.

Adam's ears turned bright red. For a moment, he looked like he was about to lash out, but instead he stomped past the boys, knocking chairs out of his way. "You're gonna lose today, Mercer. Mark my words."

"Don't listen to him," Joe said. "You're going to be fine."

"I don't know about that, but thanks for cheering me up."

"Anything for a new friend." Joe smiled. "Besides, it's not often that I get the chance to show up Adam."

"You're right," Freddy said. "Maybe everything *will* be fine."

But as the boys bent down to gather up Freddy's gear, Pete rushed into the lobby, frantically waving his arms. "It's a disaster. Someone destroyed our lucky skate!"

Chapter 3

SKATING INTO THE SPOTLIGHT

Pete was freaking out. He shouted. He jumped from side to side. He flapped his arms. He pointed back toward the locker room. What he didn't do was explain what had happened.

Frank trailed into the lobby. Spotting Joe, he walked over to the café. Frank had an excited look on his face—a look that Joe knew too well. Frank had discovered a mystery.

"Someone covered the lucky skate in paint," he said.

"It's terrible," groaned Pete, finally finding his voice. "They totally destroyed the skate, and our luck right along with it."

"This is a travesty," Freddy wailed. Whatever confidence Joe had helped him find had vanished. "First, our starting goalie gets sick. Now, someone destroyed the skate. Our luck is gone. We're doomed!"

Joe and Frank exchanged a look. They knew when a situation called for their special brand of expertise.

"Don't worry, guys," Joe said. "The Hardy brothers are on the case."

"That's right," Frank agreed. "We'll find out who tampered with your skate."

Freddy looked over at Pete. It was obvious who would take the lead here. Seeing his teammate seeking support, Pete calmed down a little and led the Hardys back toward the locker room. After collecting his gear, Freddy followed slowly behind.

"You'll really help?" Freddy asked.

"Of course," Joe responded.

"This is what we do," Frank said. "Now let's go investigate."

They filed into the locker room.

"Ugh!" Joe groaned, pinching his nose. "Bat is dat smell?"

"A locker room full of hockey gear." Pete laughed. "You get used to it pretty quick."

"Doubd dat," Joe mumbled, still holding his nose. "Bears da skade?"

"Over here," Pete said, pointing. There on a long shelf was a hockey skate. Someone had poured black paint all over it. The goo dribbled down the skate, over the shelf, and onto the floor.

Frank stepped closer to examine the mess. "Everyone, stand back. No one touch the clue. Joe, you ready?"

Joe was always ready. He pulled the clue book and pencil out of his pocket. Then he wrote down the five *W*s. That was how their dad told them to start every case.

The five *W*s were:

Who?

What?

Where?

When?

Why?

Once the boys had answers to all five *Ws*, the mystery would be solved.

"Let's do the easy ones first," Frank said. "We don't know *who* did this, but we do know *what* they did: someone poured paint on the Checkers' lucky skate."

Joe wrote that down. "We also know the *when* and *where*," he said. He wrote down *the Checkers locker room in the Bayport Ice Skating Center* for *where*. Then, after checking his watch, he wrote *Saturday, between eleven a.m. and eleven twenty a.m.* for *when*. He knew it couldn't have happened before eleven o'clock, because that was when he and Frank had arrived at the rink. It was currently eleven twenty, so that gave the culprit a maximum window of twenty minutes.

"Now comes the hard part," Frank said. "We need to find out *who* did it and *why*."

Pete raised his hands. "The *why* is easy. Someone wants us to lose."

"That's one possibility," Frank agreed. "But we can't make assumptions. We need facts, and we don't have enough of them right now."

"Maybe there're some clues outside the locker room," Joe suggested, still waving away the smell from his face.

"Good idea," Frank said. He turned to Pete and Freddy. "Anything else to add before we continue our work?"

Pete thought for a second. "Just catch whoever did this. The game starts at one o'clock. We need our luck back before then or things will end badly."

"Yeah." Freddy nodded. "I'll need all the luck I can get."

As the two hockey players started laying out their gear, Joe and Frank took their investigation into the hallway. "What's this?" Joe asked, bending down to look at something on the floor.

Frank knelt to inspect it for himself. "Looks like some paint drips. Let's see where they lead."

The two brothers followed the drips down the hall, around a corner, and back out toward the lobby. As they neared the café, the drips disappeared.

"Looks like the trail's run cold," Joe said, shrugging.

Frank glanced around. There were only a few people milling in the lobby. None of them had black paint on them. He turned his attention back to Joe. "Let's look around a little more. Maybe we missed something."

The brothers were making their way back toward

the locker room when a boy called out, "Hey, guys." It was Chet Morton, the Hardys' best friend, with his sisters, Iola and Mimi.

"Hey, Chet," Frank called back. "I thought you had soccer today."

Chet smiled at his friend. Soccer was Chet's new thing. Over the summer, he'd spent all his time on computer games. Before that, he was into robotics. Chet's interests changed as quickly as the weather and didn't usually include sports. He was only trying soccer because his mom wanted him doing something active for a change.

"Yeah. We have a scrimmage," Chet said. "But Iola is skating in the big competition today, and Mimi has the Junior Skaters' Challenge. They support me all the time, so I took a day off to come root them on."

"He's the best big brother ever," Mimi cheered.

"At least he doesn't have to stand in the rain to watch us skate like we did for his game last week," Iola complained. "He didn't even get on the field."

"You could have used an umbrella," Chet replied. "Mimi remembered to bring hers."

"As much as we'd like to listen to you three make fun of each other, we're on a case," Joe interrupted. "You didn't happen to see anyone come through here with a can of black paint, did you?"

"Sorry, guys," Chet said, shaking his head. "We just got here. You're the first people we've run into."

"What's the case?" asked Mimi.

"Someone poured paint on the Bayport Checkers' lucky skate," Frank explained.

"Eww. That's not good," said Iola. "Those hockey players are really superstitious."

"That's what Pam said," Joe replied.

"Sorry I can't help. I've got to get the girls down to their sign-ins," said Chet with a wave. "Good luck, guys. I know you'll figure out who messed with the skate."

The Hardy brothers waved back. It was nice to have their friend's confidence. It would have been nicer if they had another clue.

Too bad they didn't.

Chapter 4

FULL PRESS

"We need to get to work," Frank said. As more and more people arrived at the rink for the day's events, the chances of the Hardys missing a clue only went up.

"Let's follow the paint back toward the locker room," suggested Frank. "There'll be fewer people there, plus I want another peek at the scene of the crime."

Chants and music could be heard from the open

locker-room door as the team got ready for their game. The Checkers' coach poked his head inside and called, "Time for warm-ups."

Before Joe could say *watch out*, the whole Checkers team poured out of the locker room and streamed past the brothers. Freddy spotted the Hardys off to the side and asked, "Any luck solving the case?"

"Nothing yet," Joe admitted, watching his new friend's shoulders sag. "It's really early in our investigation."

"We're still working on it," added Frank, trying to cheer the goalie up. Freddy met Frank's eye and gave him a weak smile.

"They'll figure it out," Pete said, tapping Freddy on the shoulder. Then the two boys followed their team to the exercise room for warm-ups.

The brothers had the locker room to themselves, so they settled in for some uninterrupted investigation. The skate was still on the shelf, but someone had placed paper towels under it. There was also evidence that someone had tried to clean up the paint on the floor. Other than that, everything looked the same as when they'd left.

Joe frowned. It was never good when someone messed with a crime scene. "Looks like we're not gonna get much else from here," he grumbled. "The scene's been tampered with. What next?"

"Let's go through the timeline," suggested Frank. "Maybe that will give us something new."

"It couldn't hurt," Joe agreed. He didn't like when clues hid from them. He took pride in their ability to quickly root out the truth. With the start of the game approaching, they didn't have much time. "We entered the building right around eleven a.m. I went to grab something to eat at the café."

"And I followed Pete to the locker room. He dropped off his bag and immediately took out their lucky skate. The team gives it to the player of the game, and Pete got it last game. He said it had to be up on the shelf here before the rest of the team arrived. That's another of those superstitions Pam was talking about."

"That couldn't have taken more than a few minutes," Joe said. "What happened next?"

Frank thought for a second. He wanted to make sure he reported every detail exactly as it had happened. "Pete went into the bathroom," he continued, pointing to the shower area. Then he spun and pointed back out the door. "I offered to fill his water bottle and stepped out to the fountain for water."

"Was there anyone else in the room before you left?" asked Joe.

Frank frowned as he considered the question. "When I left, the locker room was empty."

"Okay," Joe said. "With Pete in the bathroom and you at the water fountain, our culprit had an opening."

"That seems right. There was only a short window of time for them to get in and out—just a few minutes. I was facing away from the door as I filled the bottle, so I didn't see anyone near the locker room."

"This doesn't seem to be getting us anywhere," Joe said, shaking his head. "How do we not even have a single suspect yet?"

Just then, a loud *thump* came from down the

hallway, and the boys both startled. They exchanged sheepish smiles, then stepped out to see what had created the racket. Wally was coming down the hall pushing a mop bucket, and he didn't look happy.

"I can't believe these kids," Wally grumbled to himself. "Every day, it's the same thing. These hockey players don't care who has to clean up after them."

Frank and Joe quickly stepped out of the ranting maintenance worker's way. As Wally passed into the locker room, Joe noticed something strange. He nudged Frank's arm and pointed at Wally's hand.

Peeking around the doorframe, Frank watched as Wally started to mop the floor, trying to catch a glimpse of what Joe had spotted.

"Black paint on his hands," Frank

whispered. His mind started racing. Was the answer that easy? Was Wally their culprit?

"Wait a minute. I'm remembering something. I saw Wally talking with the other team's coach when Pete and I came down to the locker room," Frank exclaimed. "They seemed pretty friendly, and there was definitely time for Wally to get into the locker room while I was filling Pete's bottle."

"What would his motivation be?" asked Joe. "He seemed friendly with Pete and Pam. Why would he ruin the team's skate, especially if he's the one cleaning up the mess?"

Joe had a point. "Maybe he did it for the other coach?" Frank offered. "If they're friends?"

"It's possible," admitted Joe. He didn't think Wally was the guy, but a good detective didn't rule anyone out without proof. And right now, proof of any kind was in short supply.

As the Hardy brothers considered this new twist in their case, Freddy suddenly came running down the hallway, eyes wide. "Come quick, guys," he managed to get out, before bending over to catch his breath.

Frank and Joe dashed after him. As they made the turn into the exercise room, the trio pulled up. Standing in front of the wall was the rest of the Checkers team. They were all talking and pointing at something that had been taped there.

The Hardy brothers stepped forward to get a closer look at whatever had captured everyone's attention—a sign.

Chapter 5

CRACK IN THE ICE

"Doomed!" Freddy wailed. "We're doomed!"

His Checkers teammates were trying to comfort the distraught goalie, but he just kept saying, "Doomed!" and stomping around in circles. Finally the coach came over and led Freddy back to the locker room.

"Why would someone do this?" Pete asked. "After all the hard work we put in to get to the championship game, we might need to forfeit?"

"That's not going to happen," said Frank confidently. "Joe and I will figure out who did this. And now we have another clue to help us catch the culprit."

Joe reached out and pulled the paper off the wall. "This note is more than a threat. It's a lead."

"Who had the opportunity to post this?" Frank asked.

Pete shook his head. "The exercise room is a public place." He was fidgeting with a hockey stick, knocking a heavy ball back and forth. "Everyone has access."

"That doesn't help us narrow down the suspect pool," Joe said. "Did you see anyone suspicious hanging around here when you came in for warm-ups?"

Pete made figure eights with the ball while he tried to think back. "Nope. Nothing seemed out of the ordinary. There're a lot of people here today, and I was focused on getting ready to play."

Frank and Joe looked around the exercise room. They didn't see any other clues. Their investigation wasn't getting any easier.

SNAP!

All three boys jumped as Pete's stick snapped in half.

"What the—" Pete shook his head. "The bad luck is getting worse!"

Frank knelt to examine the blade of the stick, turning it so that he could see the break point more clearly. "Look here, Joe. I think someone messed with Pete's stick."

Joe took the blade from his brother. "There's a notch! It's definitely been tampered with."

Pete looked at the broken shaft in his hands. "Right here," he said, indicating a worn-down area. "I think someone rubbed a skate against the shaft to weaken it."

"Could that damage have happened in a game or practice?" asked Frank. "Maybe someone's skate blade glanced off your stick while you were playing?"

Pete shook his head. "Not possible. I check my stick after every game. You don't want it to break during play. That leaves your team a man down."

Joe nodded. That made a lot of sense. "Where do you keep your stick before games?" he asked.

"Outside the locker room, in the stick rack, along with the rest of the team's." Pete's eyes went wide. "The other sticks . . ."

The three boys rushed to the stick rack. Pete grabbed a stick and showed Frank and Joe what to look for. Working together, they quickly made it through the whole rack.

"They all seem fine," Frank said. He turned to Pete as a new thought struck him. "I think they were targeting you."

"Makes sense," said Joe. "Pete's the best player. *And* he has those superstitions."

"Not superstitions. It's a process," Pete corrected. "It gets me ready to play. Sports science says that if you do the same thing before each game, it puts you in the right mindset for success."

"I'm not sure sports science would agree that touching a smelly skate is part of a good process," replied Joe. "But it does look like you're the target of these attacks."

"Who would want you to lose?" Frank asked.

"Anyone rooting for the Snipers," said Pete. "Or against us."

"They'd need to have access to the locker room, the stick rack, and the exercise room," Frank added.

"Pretty much anyone can get back here," Pete said. "It's not like we have a security guard."

"So *anyone* would have had the opportunity to sneak in and tamper with your stick," concluded Joe.

"Maybe we can try to narrow down the pool," Frank said.

Joe thought that was a good idea. "Let's make a

list." Since this was part of their usual process of figuring out suspects, he was ready. He pulled out the clue book, and under *Who?* wrote *Suspects*. Underneath that, he wrote *Adam Ackerman*.

"What makes you think Adam did this?" Frank asked as Joe handed him the clue book. "I haven't even seen him here."

"Unfortunately, I have," Joe said. "He's upset because he didn't make the Checkers. Plus, he said

he was supporting the Snipers. That's two good reasons for him to make our suspect list."

"Well, we should probably add Wally, then," Frank said. "He's friendly with the other team's coach, had black paint on his hand, and was grumbling about the Checkers making a mess in the locker room."

Joe frowned as he considered other possible culprits. "Is there a chance it could be someone else?" he finally asked, glancing at Pete, who just shrugged.

Frank nodded. "We need to keep that as a possibility. I'll go talk to Adam. He might be more willing to give something up if I'm the one doing the asking."

"Yeah, I'm okay not seeing him again," Joe said. "I'll go find Wally."

With that decided, the boys went off in search of their suspects, and Pete went to rejoin the team in the locker room. Luckily, Frank found Adam in the first place he looked: watching figure skaters on rink one.

Frank approached him cautiously. He knew from

past experience that you didn't want to set Adam off by throwing out accusations. "Hey, Adam. Mind if I ask you something?"

"Whatever it is, I had nothing to do with it, Hardy," Adam snapped. "I've been sitting here ever since I ran into your runt of a brother."

"You didn't happen to go down to the locker

rooms to look for any of your friends?" asked Frank.

"Didn't need to," Adam said with a sneer. "I always watch the skaters before games so I can rate their falls." He held up a sheet of paper he'd been writing on. "If anyone wants to say hi, they know where to find me."

Frank took out the paper the threat had been scrawled on. "You didn't happen to see anyone put this up, did you? We found it hanging on the wall in the exercise room." He pointed down the hall to where the Checkers had been gathered earlier.

"Nah. I've just been sitting here watching skaters fall down. I haven't been paying attention to what goes on off the ice."

Frank was inclined to believe Adam's alibi. Besides, the writing on the note didn't match the writing on Adam's paper. They'd need to cross him off their list.

Hopefully, Joe would have better luck with Wally.

Chapter 6

A MISSED SHOT

While Frank had no trouble finding Adam, Joe wasn't having as much success in his search for Wally. He checked the café, rinks one *and* two, and the exercise room, and he even went back to the locker room. But Joe couldn't find the elusive maintenance man anywhere.

The whole time he was searching, more and more people were streaming into the rink to watch the big events. As Joe passed the exercise room on his way into the lobby for the second time, he noticed the clock on the wall said twelve fifteen. The game started in forty-five minutes. He was running out of time.

Joe was just about to give up when a door at the end of the hall marked EMPLOYEES ONLY swung open, and Wally came strolling out.

Finally, Joe thought. He rushed over to catch the maintenance worker before he could get away again.

"Hi, Wally. I'm Joe Hardy. Mind if I ask you a few questions?"

"As long as you make it quick. I've got to cut rink two in five minutes."

"Cut the what?" Joe asked, looking around for a giant pair of scissors.

"Cut the ice," Wally corrected. "It's my way of saying resurface the rink."

"This'll only take a second," Joe promised. "I'm looking into who poured paint on that skate in the Checkers' locker room. You didn't happen to see anything, did you?"

"Kids," grumbled Wally. He shook his head. "They've got no respect for anything around them *or* the people who clean up their messes. Unfortunately, I wasn't near the locker room when it happened. I dropped the visitor's room key off with the Snipers coach and went to cut ice on rink one. I'd just finished when I heard about that skate prank. It's not the first one of their messes I've had to clean up."

Joe made a note in the clue book. "What do you mean by that?" he asked.

"Those hockey players like to play practical jokes on each other," explained Wally. "This is probably just another one of their tricks."

Based on how the team had reacted, Joe wasn't sure this was a prank, but he wrote it down anyway. It was worth looking into. "Would anyone have seen you cutting the ice?"

"If they were looking." Wally gestured out the café window toward the rink, then narrowed his eyes. "Am I a suspect in your little investigation?"

"Well," Joe started. "You do have black paint on your hands."

Wally turned his palms to examine the black splotches, then nodded and smiled at Joe. "That I

do, young man. Good job noticing it, but I got this cleaning up that mess. I tried to use some paper towels. I even put some under the skate. Then I tried my trusty mop bucket. It just spread the paint around. I think I'm going to need some paint thinner to get it all." He paused for a moment, then shook his head sadly. "Whoever made that mess sure didn't think about how I'd have to clean it up."

Joe glanced at Wally's hands again. The paint could have come from cleaning. And when Joe looked closer, he noticed that there was paint on

Wally's knees and shoes as well, like he'd knelt or stepped in it. There hadn't been any footprints or knee marks when they'd first looked at the scene.

"Well, like I said, I gotta go cut some ice." Wally grinned. "Hope you catch the culprit. When you do, you tell them I don't appreciate them making that mess."

"I will," Joe told him. They said goodbye, and then Wally continued on his way toward the rink.

Joe believed Wally's story, but just to be safe, he decided to retrace the maintenance worker's steps from rink one to the locker room. Maybe Wally had time to tamper with the skate *and* cut the ice on rink one?

Unfortunately, that idea was quickly proven wrong. Rink one was on the opposite side of the lobby. Unless cutting the ice only took a few minutes, it was way too far for Wally to have done both. As Joe was walking back to find Frank, he noticed Pam Peterson sitting against the lobby wall. She looked upset.

Joe prided himself on being a good friend. Since

he wasn't getting anywhere with his part of the investigation, it wouldn't hurt to take a minute or two to see if he could help. "Hey, Pam," he said. "Everything okay?"

Pam looked up. Her eyes were a little puffy and red, as if she'd been crying. "I'm fine," she responded, in a tone that definitely said she was *not* fine.

Joe knew that people didn't always say what they meant. He sat down next to her. "Do you want to talk about it?"

"Thanks." Pam sniffed. "But I think I'll be all right. My parents called to say they're running late.

And I'm worried about the skating competition."

"Is it a big one?" asked Joe. He didn't really know anything about figure skating.

Pam nodded. "It's only the FSSIC's second-biggest event of the year."

"The FS what?"

"The Figure Skating Society of International Competitions," Pam explained. "They're one of the governing bodies for figure skating. This competition is where they identify skaters for things like the Olympic programs or school scholarships. All kinds of stuff. The winners go on to nationals."

"Wow," Joe said, impressed. "That's pretty cool. And you're worried about how you'll do?"

"Something like that," Pam murmured. "Not that it matters. No one's coming to watch. Everyone will be over at Pete's game."

"Really? It looked like a lot of people were watching the figure skaters."

"They don't stay." Pam looked at the ground.

"They don't?" Joe asked, confused.

"Figure-skating routines only last three and a half

minutes. That's it. Then you're done, win or lose. We practice just as much as hockey players. More, even. But they get ninety minutes of ice time. We get less than four. It's so not fair."

"What happens the rest of the time?" asked Joe. "Do they cut the ice between each skater?"

"Nah. They only cut after a whole group goes," Pam explained. "It would take way too long if they did it after each routine."

Joe's interest was piqued. Maybe this conversation would end up helping his investigation after all. "How long does it take to cut the ice?"

Pam thought for a moment. "Around ten or fifteen minutes if you wait till the ice freezes. Otherwise, you're skating around in a swamp."

If that was true, then there was no way that Wally could be the saboteur. He didn't have time. Wally was innocent.

Chapter

7

GETTING COLD FEET

Joe thanked Pam for the information and wished her luck in her competition. After hearing about all the work she'd put in, he really hoped he'd be able to see her perform her routine. "If we can solve this mystery in time, I'll be by to watch you skate," he told her.

Pam thanked him but didn't make eye contact. *She must be really concerned about the competition,* thought Joe. But the clock was ticking. If he wanted to keep his promise, he couldn't lose any more time

48 ⇄

on this case. He needed to find Frank and share what he'd learned.

Frank had just finished up speaking with Adam. Joe watched as the big bully stalked off toward the restrooms. Kids, and even their parents, hurried to get out of the way as Adam stormed by.

"Any luck with Adam?" Joe asked as he came to Frank's side. "Please tell me he did it."

"Nah. I'm pretty sure it couldn't have been him. Besides, the handwriting doesn't match Adam's. Sorry, Joe. Adam's not our guy."

"That's a bummer." Joe groaned before crossing Adam's name off the suspect list. "I was hoping he'd be the culprit this time. One of these days, we'll catch him in the act."

"What about Wally?" asked Frank, nudging his brother out of his wishful dreaming.

"Turns out we're on thin ice there, too," Joe said with a sigh. "Wally isn't really friends with the Snipers' coach. He was just giving him a locker-room key. Then he went to cut ice. That's where he was when the Checkers' lucky skate was messed with. Pam says that it takes at least ten minutes to do the entire rink. Wally wouldn't have had time to do both."

Joe put a big line through Wally's name. "Unfortunately, that was our last suspect."

They'd hit a wall again.

"Come on, Joe." Frank motioned for his brother to follow him over to a bench in the lobby. "We can't give up now. That's not the Hardy way."

"I know," Joe said. "It's just . . . I'd love for one of these mysteries to be easy. You know, pull the mask off and there's Old Man Jenkins. Then we could go for cake."

"What are you talking about?" Frank was pretty sure his brother was rambling.

"Nothing," Joe said, waving it off. "I just saw those kids over at the birthday table, and now I want cake."

"Tell you what," said Frank. "Let's brainstorm some suspects, and when we catch the culprit, I'll find you a snack."

Joe immediately perked up. "Okay. Who else could it be? A player from the other team?"

"I don't think so. Their locker room was right by the water fountain, so I would have seen them. And how would they have known which stick was Pete's?"

Frank made some good points. "Okay. So not them. Who else?" Joe asked. Then he had a thought. "Wally said the Checkers were in some kind of prank war. Could they have done this themselves?"

Frank frowned. "I would hope not, but we should check it out. Maybe there's someone on the team who doesn't want the game to go on." He paused. "I know he's your friend, but Freddy seems to be trying to avoid playing. Do you think it could be him?"

Joe was hesitant to make Freddy a suspect. "I'm not sure he had time to dump the paint. He was with me at the café."

Frank considered that. Freddy definitely had access to the stick rack, and he would have known which one was Pete's. But would Freddy have had enough time to tamper with the skate and still get back to the café? "Could he have done it before meeting you?" Frank asked.

Joe shrugged. Freddy *was* worried about the

game. Plus, he'd been acting strange all day. With a sigh, Joe admitted it was possible. "I guess we should add him to our list of suspects."

"If Bayport forfeits, Freddy would be off the hook," Frank reasoned. "There's even a chance that the game would get rescheduled when the regular goalie could play. I think it's at least worth finding Freddy and confirming his alibi."

"You're right," said Joe. "I just don't like it. The idea of Freddy sabotaging his own team tastes like black licorice. Yuck."

"What's with you and food today?"

"The birthday party has a piñata," Joe said, motioning toward the café area. "It's got me thinking of candy."

"Come on." Frank laughed. "Let's find Freddy."

It didn't take long to locate the goalie. He was bouncing a ball off a wall near the Checkers' locker room.

"Hey, Freddy," Joe called. "What're you doing?"

"It's a pregame warm-up," Freddy explained. "You've got to keep your eyes on the ball or you miss

it, just like trying to stop a puck. You track its path, figure out where it's going, what it will do, and then grab it before it gets into the goal."

"Kind of like we do with suspects," offered Joe. "Keep your eyes on them. Track them down. Catch them before they do something again."

"Exactly," Freddy said, catching the ball and launching it again.

"That's kind of why we're here," said Joe, his eyes following the ball. "We need to follow up on some leads."

Freddy stopped his warm-up. "Do you have a good suspect?" he asked, excited.

"No one in particular," Frank cut in. "We're still trying to rule people out."

"Which brings us to you," Joe said carefully.

Freddy looked confused. "How can I help?"

"We just need to rule you out," explained Joe. "It's part of the process."

Freddy nodded. "I understand. Check all the angles. Make sure nothing gets past you."

"Exactly." Joe smiled.

"Can you walk us through where you were from eleven o'clock until you met up with Joe?" asked Frank.

"Sure. My dad dropped me off out front just after eleven," Freddy began. "Once I came inside, I headed right to the café. I always get a candy bar and an orange energy drink before a game. That's when I bumped into Joe."

"You didn't go to the locker room first?" Frank asked.

"The café is right in front of the entrance. It doesn't make sense to go all the way to the locker room and then come back. Besides, if I had, I would have left my equipment there. That stuff is heavy. In fact, the ticket lady held the door for me when I walked into the rink. I bet she could tell you when I came in and which direction I went."

"He did have a full load of stuff when we bumped into each other," Joe added.

"What about these pranks we've heard about?" asked Frank. "Could someone else on the team be playing jokes?"

"No way!" Freddy said. "The rink complained to Coach last week. He told us that anyone playing another prank is off the team. Besides, no one would ever mess with the lucky skate. That wouldn't be funny. It would hurt the entire team. Everyone's worked way too hard to reach the championship to do something like that."

"Thanks, Freddy," Frank said. "We'll let you get back to tracking pucks."

"Good luck!" called Joe.

"Good luck to you, too," the goalie offered.

"We're gonna need it," Joe muttered, looking up at the clock.

Less than thirty minutes to game time, and they were out of suspects . . . again.

Chapter 8

WINNERS NEVER QUIT

Frank and Joe went back out to the café. Not only was it a good place to think, but that was where the food was, and Joe was still hungry.

Hungry, but indecisive.

"It's not rocket science," Frank said, crossing his arms. "Just pick something."

Joe glared back at his brother. "I wanted a Super Chunk, but they're all out."

Frank rolled his eyes. They had work to do and Joe was being picky about candy bars.

"Hey, guys," Chet called. "How's the investigation going?"

"About as good as my ability to get a snack," replied Joe. "Can you believe they're out of Super Chunks?"

"Not sure what I can do to help the investigation," Chet said, "but I always bring an extra something to eat." He pulled a Super Chunk bar out of his backpack, broke off a piece, and handed it to Joe.

"Thanks, Chet," said Joe, a huge smile lighting up his face. "This is the first good news we've had all day."

"No progress, then?" Chet asked.

"Every suspect we've come up with has an alibi," Frank told him.

"Even Adam," mumbled Joe before popping the piece of chocolate into his mouth.

"Sometimes, when I'm stuck on a problem, it helps if I do something else for a bit," Chet said. "Then, when I go back to my original problem, I can come at it with fresh eyes."

"That makes a lot of sense," said Frank.

Joe moaned. "Plus, this mystery is making my head hurt."

"Are you sure it's not that candy bar making your head hurt? You did scarf it down pretty quick."

Joe frowned at his brother. Then he pointed at the ice. "Isn't that Mimi?"

"Yeah. She's up next in the Junior Skaters' Challenge," Chet responded. "Want to watch with me?"

Frank nodded. "It just might be the distraction we need to help us figure out this case."

"Absolutely," agreed Joe. "I was talking to Pam about figure skating earlier. It sounds really difficult."

"Just skating is hard enough on its own," Chet told the brothers. "Then you add in all the spins and jumps. For her age, Mimi makes it look easy. She's super talented. Even better than Iola. Just don't tell *her* I said that."

Joe flashed Chet a grin. "I'll keep it a secret for another bite of your Super Chunk."

Chet handed Joe another piece, and the three boys sat down to watch Mimi. Deep bass music filled the rink as Mimi started her routine. She effortlessly switched from gliding forward to backward. She spun. She leaped. The boys were riveted by her every twist and turn.

As the music reached its crescendo, Mimi skated faster and faster. Then, with a final thump of bass, she stopped.

"Wow," Frank said.

"Yeah, wow," added Joe. "That was amazing."

"Told you she was good." Chet beamed. "At first she didn't even want to skate. But she would always come watch Iola practice. The coach finally got her to give it a try. And when Mimi got on the ice, she took to it like a fish to water."

"Frozen water," Joe joked.

"Nice." Chet laughed. "You know what's interesting? Sometimes talent turns up in the last place you'd expect it. Like Mimi being an amazing skater versus my skill with games and computers."

"Or me being smart and Frank being dumb," Joe said, cracking up.

"Very funny." Frank wasn't laughing. "Maybe you could turn that big brain of yours toward finding us another suspect. We *are* still on a case."

Joe sobered up quickly. Frank had a point. "Who else could it be?"

That was when Pete came storming out of the rink shop with a new hockey stick. "I can't believe it! Someone mashed up all the black tape into a big sticky ball, and the shop doesn't have any more for my new stick."

"Can't you use white?" asked Chet, peering from

the café area through the shop window. There were big stacks of white tape next to smaller ones of green, blue, red, and a few other colors.

"I've never played with any other color," Pete complained. "It has to be *black*. Black tape helps hide the puck. Any other color won't be the same."

"Slow down," said Joe, pulling out the clue book. "You said something about tape being mashed together?"

"Yeah. I needed to tape my new stick and I couldn't find the roll I keep in my bag. I went to the store to get some, but they don't have any. Mike, the guy who runs the shop, said he stepped out for a minute, and when he returned, the black tape was all mushed together. Destroyed."

"Sounds like another clue," Joe said, writing down what had happened in the notebook.

"Right. Let's go see what happened," Frank suggested, before heading to speak to Mike.

The other boys followed Frank into the rink shop. "Excuse me," said Frank, looking around. "Did something strange just happen in here?"

"Yeah, dude," the confused shop attendant responded. "It's, like, the strangest thing. Somehow, all my black tape got stomped together." He plopped a huge gob of black muck onto the counter—more than a dozen rolls of black stick tape had been mashed up into one sticky mess.

"Was anyone in the shop when you left? Or when you returned?" Frank asked.

"There've been a lot of people in and out today, but no one was here when I stepped away," Mike told them. "Technically, I'm not supposed to leave the

shop, but I kinda had to go, if you get my meaning."

Everyone got his meaning.

"Did you lock the door while you were gone?" asked Joe. If the door had been locked, that would definitely limit their suspects.

"Oh, yeah. Like, no," Mike responded, shrinking down in his chair.

"This is a disaster," Pete wailed. "I'll never be able to score now. Our luck is totally gone. I don't think I should play."

"You can't give up," said Frank as confidently as he could. "You have to play. The Checkers are depending on you."

"It's not going to make a difference who plays," Pete replied, sounding deflated. "We'll never win. And, besides, with our luck gone, what if something worse happens?"

"Are you really that superstitious?" Joe asked.

"A friend of mine tried to play when all the luck was telling him not to," Pete told them. "His skate blade broke. He fell and sprained his wrist. He couldn't play for three months!"

"We'll figure this out," promised Frank. "In the meantime, you need to get your head in the game."

"I can't take the chance," Pete said. "If our luck doesn't change quick, I need to sit out."

"Everyone, into the locker room," called Pete's coach from the lobby. "Game time in ten minutes."

"Pete, you go get ready," Frank told his friend. "Joe and I will handle this."

"Ten minutes to solve this case? That's not much time," Joe whispered to his brother as they walked out of the shop.

Frank looked more determined than ever. "It'll have to be enough."

A MAJOR BREAKTHROUGH

As the boys walked Pete to the locker room, he still seemed worried about playing. "I'm not sure I can do this," he told Frank. "Maybe I'm better off just watching from the stands with you guys."

"You need to get ready to play," Frank calmly urged him. "We'll figure out who's been messing with your luck before the game starts."

"Okay," agreed Pete reluctantly. "I'll get dressed

and ready, but I'm not taking the ice unless the team's luck returns."

"We've got this," Joe told him with less confidence than his brother. "The Hardy brothers are on the case, and we always catch our man. Or woman. Suspect. We always catch our suspect."

"You're not helping," Frank said, glaring at his brother. He turned back to Pete. "We'll figure this out. I promise."

"Thanks!" Pete said before slipping into the locker room.

"So," Joe started. "How exactly are we going to figure this out, Mr. Promise Maker? We don't have any suspects, remember?"

"That's easy," said Frank. "We'll walk back through all the information we do have and see where it leads us. There has to be something we've missed."

"Of course." Joe crossed his arms. "Some clue will miraculously pop out of nowhere and help us figure out the mystery."

"Still not helping," Frank snapped. "Come on,

Joe. We've done this a hundred times. Focus. What do we know?"

"Okay." Joe took out the clue book. "Here are the facts we have."

1. Between eleven a.m. and eleven twenty a.m., someone snuck into the Checkers' locker room and poured black paint on the team's lucky skate.

2. Sometime after the last practice, and before the team went out for warm-ups, Pete's hockey stick was cut with a skate blade. The cut caused it to break when Pete tried to use it.

3. A sign was put up in the exercise room saying the Checkers needed to forfeit the game to get their luck back. Everyone had access to the room.

4. All the black tape in the rink shop was mushed together. Only the black. No other colors.

5. Suspects: Adam, Wally, Freddy

Joe flipped around in the clue book. "That's all the facts we have."

"Okay," Frank said, a small smile forming on his lips. "We may not need anything more than that."

"Really?" asked Joe. "Do you see something I don't?"

"There's a connection between all the incidents. Whoever our suspect is, they know a lot about the Checkers. More specifically, they know a lot about Pete."

"I'm not sure I follow," Joe said.

"First, they knew how superstitious the team is," Frank explained. "They also knew those superstitions center around the lucky skate."

"Yeah. They also knew which stick was Pete's. That means they've seen him with it or watched him put it in the rack."

"Exactly." Frank pumped his fist, getting more excited as they pieced the details together. "Finally, they knew that Pete uses *only* black stick tape."

"So our suspect knows Pete pretty well. Or they've spent a lot of time around the rink?"

"That's my thought," Frank agreed. "I've just got one more thing to check out, and then I think we can call this case solved."

As the two boys approached the stands, they could see the team gathered next to the rink door, waiting to go on the ice. The big game would be starting in just a few minutes.

Pete was pacing in front of the doorway. "Did you figure it out?" he asked.

"We're really close," Frank assured him.

Pete wrung his hands together. "I can't do this. Without my luck, I just can't do this."

Freddy was standing off to the other side. The poor goalie was so nervous, his glasses were fogging up.

Joe walked over and put a hand on his shoulder. "Everything's going to be okay. We're really close to a breakthrough."

"You are?" Freddy looked up hopefully. "What did you figure out?"

"Just one more thing to check," Frank said as he joined them. "Give me a minute to test my theory." With that, he turned and walked toward the ice.

"Where's he going?" Freddy asked.

Joe shrugged. "No idea." He looked around, trying to figure out his brother's plan. "Guess I should find out what's going on, though. I'll be cheering for you guys!"

Joe dashed after his brother, racing up the tunnel. As he approached the ice, Joe could see Frank a little ways down the wall, speaking with Pam. She was pacing frantically, twisting her shoes into the ground, and rubbing her arms.

As Joe approached, Pam shook her head. Once. Twice. A third time. She looked miserable. *Her nerves have got her all worked up,* Joe thought.

Then his eyes focused on her shoes again. There were streaks of something across the toes.

Was that why she was walking awkwardly?

He glanced over at Frank. One look at his brother's face, and Joe knew Frank had confirmed something big.

BZZZZZZZZZ!

The buzzer rang, signaling the teams to take the ice.

"I know what happened," Frank said. "We have to tell Pete so he'll play."

The brothers dashed over to the doorway. The team was just about to go on, but Pete was standing off to the side. He kept glancing back to the locker room.

"You'll be fine," Frank said, panting. "I figured it out."

"Really?" Freddy had walked up to Pete's side. "You know what happened?"

"Frank does," confirmed Joe. "If he says you're good, then you're good. Nothing to worry about."

"Are you sure?" Pete asked.

"Just go out and win the game," Frank told him confidently. "I guarantee your luck will be back. I know exactly what happened."

THE HARDY BOYS—and
YOU!

CAN YOU SOLVE THE MYSTERY OF THE BAD LUCK SKATE?

1. Grab a piece of paper and write your answers down. Or just turn the page to find out what happened!

2. Frank and Joe made a list of suspects. Can you think of anyone they didn't include?

3. A good detective looks for a motive, or a reason that someone commits a crime. What do you think the motive was for someone to tamper with the Checkers' luck?

4. Which clues helped you to solve this mystery? Write them down. Was one more helpful than the rest? Circle that clue.

Chapter 10

HE SHOOTS AND . . . SCORES

The scoreboard clock showed ten seconds to go in the game. The score was 4–3. The Checkers led the Snipers by one.

Frank and Joe were on the edge of their seats as around them the crowd roared in the stands. A countdown started: "Ten, nine, eight . . ."

Deep in their own zone, the Snipers' best player took the puck from the corner. He streaked up the ice.

Pete dove to slap the puck off his stick, but number eighty-six deked past Pete's outstretched arms. The talented Sniper flew into the Checkers' end.

"Seven, six, five . . . ," the crowd screamed.

No defensemen stood in the Snipers' way. It was just him and the goalie. Freddy stood tall at the top of his crease. The Sniper faked right. He slid the puck left.

"Four, three, two . . . ," the crowd chanted.

He shot!

Freddy slid across the goal mouth. His glove snapped up toward the puck. And he grabbed it! Right as . . .

BZZZZZZZZ!

The buzzer signaled the end of the game.

The Checkers streamed out onto the ice. Players hugged one another and cheered.

As the celebration calmed down, the players got in line for the postgame handshake. Frank and Joe looked on from the stands. "That was a great game," Joe said.

"It was," agreed Frank. "Now it's time for us to bring our game to a close too."

On the ice, a trophy was brought out for the Checkers. The team gathered around it for photos.

"They're going to be off the ice in a minute," Joe warned. "And even though you finally have a suspect, we don't have anything linking them to all the crimes."

"That's where you're wrong," Frank told him. "Give me a minute and I'll prove it."

Joe didn't like the drama of waiting, but he was willing to let his brother have this one. Besides, it gave him a few more minutes to figure things out for himself.

As Joe pondered how to link their new suspect to the other clues, Freddy made his way off the ice.

Joe paused in chewing over the case and rushed up to his new friend. "You played out of your mind," he told Freddy. "I knew you could do it. That save right at the buzzer? That's the real reason the Checkers won the championship. You should be proud of yourself."

"I played okay," Freddy admitted. "The rest of

the team really stepped up, though. That's why we won."

Just then Pete came off the ice, carrying the trophy. "Great game," said Frank.

"We managed to hold them off," Pete said with a grin. "All thanks to my man Freddy here."

Freddy blushed. "Hey, you said you figured out who was messing with our luck?"

"Yeah." Pete set the big trophy down. "What really happened?"

Frank scanned the crowd, his expression relaxing when he spotted the person he'd been looking for. He turned back to Pete. "Before I answer, someone's been waiting to congratulate you. How about you give Pam a hug to celebrate the big win first?"

Pete shrugged and went over to his sister. As he approached, his arms out wide, she flinched away.

"Whoa!" Pete exclaimed, jumping back. "I didn't mean to scare you. Is everything okay?"

Pam looked at the ground. She tried to hide her arms behind her back. "Not exactly," she admitted.

"It's okay," Frank told her. "I know what

happened. But it would probably be best if Pete heard it from you."

Pam shrank down. She knew that Frank was right. Sighing, she pointed to her shoes. They still had bits of tape on them, and her arms had spots of glue up to her elbows.

"I'm so sorry," she whispered. "I thought that if you forfeited the game, maybe someone would come watch *me* skate for a change."

"You're the one who poured paint on the skate?" asked Pete. "And cut my stick?"

Pam finally looked up at him. "Everyone always talks about how great you are because you play hockey. No one pays any attention to my figure skating. Who wants to go through all the effort, put on all the extra clothing, just to watch a few minutes of a routine?"

Everyone was staring at Pam. Pete shook his head. "You think I like all this attention? Sure, it's nice when we actually win, but anytime the team isn't doing great, I'm the one everyone points to. I'd gladly step out of the spotlight if that was an option."

"It's easier to step out of the light than step into it," Pam complained. She stood in front of her brother, her shoulders slumped. "I really am sorry that I caused you so much trouble. My plan didn't even work. It just got everyone angry and me totally freaked out right before I need to skate." She turned to leave.

"Pam, wait," Pete called, reaching out to her. "I think you're an amazing figure skater. I'm sorry I haven't let you know that before. I really should have. How about I drop my stuff off in the locker room and then I'll come watch your routine?"

"How about we all go?" Joe suggested.

Pam's face lit up. There was a flash of hope in her eyes. "Really? You're not mad at me?"

"No one was hurt," Pete reasoned. "The team won, and I learned something important about my sister. I think we can let it slide this time. Just don't mess with our mojo again."

"I won't," Pam promised with a grin.

"Looks like we can put this case on ice," said Joe.

Frank put his arm around his brother's shoulder.

"It's a good thing you're a great detective, because you would never make it as a comedian."

The boys all had a good laugh as they made their way to the figure-skating rink. When it was Pam's turn to take the ice, everyone was there to cheer. Even Pam's parents and Wally. But Pete cheered the loudest.